Copyright © 1997 by Siphano
Translation copyright © 1998 by Orchard Books. Translated by Dominic Barth.
First American Edition 1998 published by Orchard Books. First published in France in 1997 by Siphano.

Orchard Books, 95 Madison Avenue, New York, NY 10016

Manufactured in the United States of America. Printed by Barton Press, Inc.
Bound by Horowitz/Rae. Book design by Mina Greenstein.
The text of this book is set in 20 point Veljovic Book.
The illustrations are watercolor reproduced in full color. 10 9 8 7 6 5 4 3 2 1

Library of Congress Cataloging-in-Publication Data
Bassède, Francine. [Boutique de Georges à la plage. English]
George's store at the shore / by Francine Bassède. — 1st American ed.   p. cm.
Summary: George and Mary bring out items to sell at George's store at the beach, counting from
one to ten as they set out the merchandise.
ISBN O-531-30083-8 (trade: alk. paper)—ISBN 0-531-33083-4 (lib. bdg. : alk. paper)
[1. Stores, Retail—Fiction. 2. Seashore—Fiction. 3. Counting.] I. Title.
PZ7.B29285Ge 1998 [E]—dc21 97-38282

GEORGE'S STORE
at the SHORE

by Francine Bassède

Orchard Books / New York

All summer long,
George gets up early.
He must get his store
at the beach ready,
with the help of his
friend, Mary.

First he carries
an umbrella. Mary
props it against the
door of the shop.

Next, two nets,
very useful for
catching fish,
crabs, and
sea urchins.

One, two...
One, two...
One, two, three
ducky floaty things:
green, blue, and red.

George brings four
beach balls, and Mary
arranges them on the
floor of the store.

"Mary, watch your claws,"
he warns.

Next, five striped
sailor shirts of cotton,
soft and cool.

What a balancing act!
George brings six pails.
Mary arranges them
on the top shelf.

A hat is indispensable
at the beach. Mary
hangs seven for
the shop.

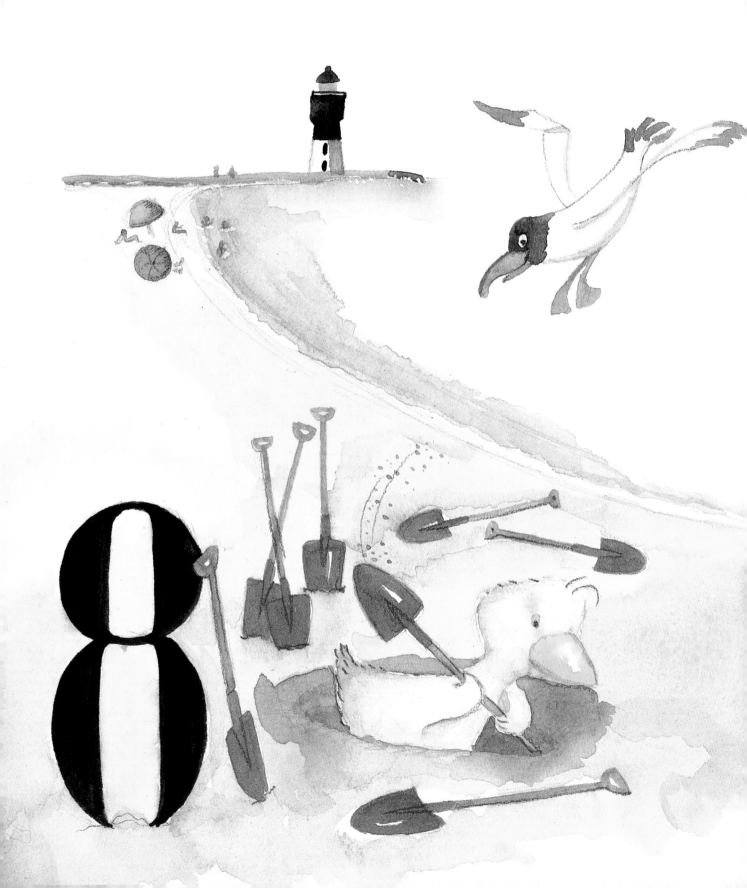

Eight shovels for
making deep holes and
tall sand castles.

A glass of freshly
squeezed orange juice!
Very tasty in the fresh sea air—
there are nine.

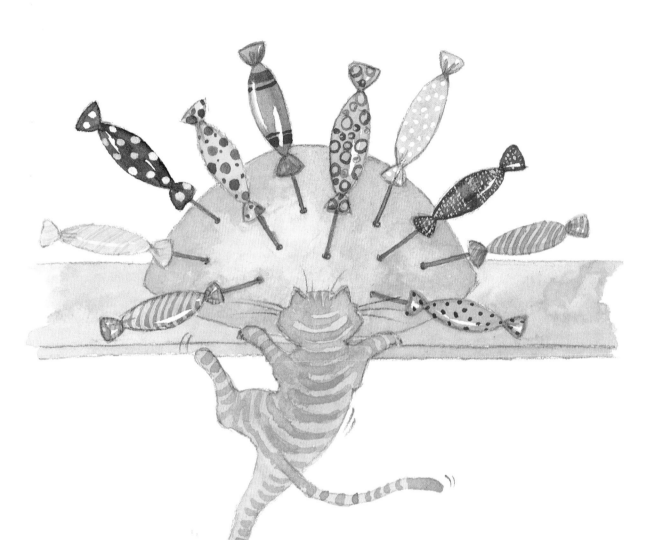

And finally, sweets!
Ten lollipops, useful while daydreaming,
each a different flavor: strawberry, lemon,
mint, chocolate, caramel, licorice, honey,
apricot, raspberry, and black currant.

A fine assortment.

The store is open.
George and Mary
are ready. It won't
be long before
customers arrive!